Understanding
AIDS

Understanding
AIDS

by Ethan A. Lerner, M.D., Ph.D.

Lerner Publications Company
Minneapolis

The author is grateful to Diane L. Sacks for encouragement during the writing of this book and especially to Theresa Early for her detailed and careful editing of the manuscript.

The author is a Lucille P. Markey Scholar and this work was supported by a grant from the Lucille P. Markey Charitable Trust.

Cover and inside illustrations by Mark Wilken

Contents

To the children with AIDS,
and to their families

Introduction

AIDS is a new disease. It was discovered in 1981. Since AIDS is caused by a **virus,** it is an **infectious** disease, which means that people catch it from other people. The reason that AIDS is talked about so much is that so many people have caught the AIDS virus and died.

Most people will not catch the virus which causes AIDS. Of those people who do catch this virus, many will develop AIDS. In people who do develop AIDS, some problems caused by the disease can be controlled. Unfortunately, there is no cure for AIDS yet.

The stories in this book provide examples of who is and who is not at risk for catching the virus which causes AIDS. You will meet people who could catch AIDS, and some who have caught AIDS, both in this book and in the real world. This book will help you understand what it is like to have AIDS. You will learn that it is usually safe to be around someone with AIDS. When you finish this book, you should know why your chances of getting AIDS are very small.

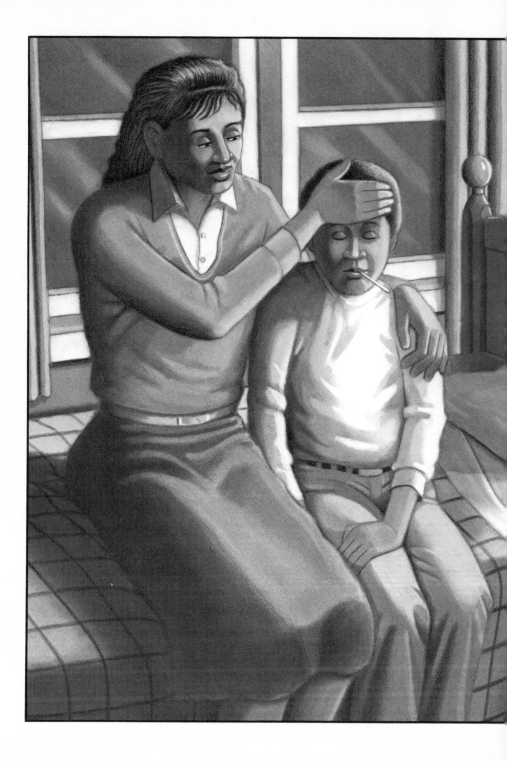

1
Swollen Glands

"You'll be late for school, Tommy Sanders," Mom yelled from downstairs.

School was about the last thing on my mind. I wasn't sure if I would ever make it back to school, I felt so bad. My throat was sore and I ached all over.

"Mom, I don't feel well," I managed to say from my bed. Mom must have heard me because a minute later she came upstairs to find out what the story was. She put her hand on my forehead and quickly drew it away.

She said, "Tommy, I think you're sick. I'll be back with a thermometer."

My temperature was high, 103.8°. That settled it. I was not going to school. Instead, Mom called Doctor Paul to make an appointment at his office that day.

There were kids of all ages waiting in Doctor Paul's office. Finally it was my turn to see the doctor.

He asked me how I felt and I said, "Lousy." He looked in my eyes, ears, runny nose, and sore throat. He seemed impressed with my throat because he even had my mother take a look. Then he stuck a long Q-tip down my throat to do a throat culture. It made me gag—yuck. Next he felt my neck and said, "Tommy, these little lumps and bumps on your neck are swollen **lymph glands**. Lymph glands act like filters and they swell up when they are filtering an infection away. I think you have strep throat, which means that a little creature called streptococcus has infected your throat. You will have to take penicillin for it."

"Oh, good," I said. "I had penicillin when I had an earache and it tasted really good."

Two days later, my fever was gone and I went back to school. Before class everyone asked how I was. I said, "Oh, I just had a little strep throat and some really big lymph glands. I had to take penicillin for it."

"Does that mean you have AIDS?" asked Mary Silvers, the know-it-all in the front row.

"What's AIDS?" I asked.

"It's something that queers get," yelled Louis Ratner.

Our teacher, Mr. Rutherford, took control. "No, Tommy does not have AIDS."

"But AIDS is a very important new disease caused by

a certain virus." Mr. Rutherford went to the black-board. "AIDS stands for **acquired immunodeficiency syndrome**," he said, writing out those big words. "The words *acquired* and *syndrome* are easy. *Acquire* means to get, so AIDS is something you catch from someone. *Syndrome* means a pattern of problems. At first, doctors didn't know what the AIDS virus looked like. All they could see was the pattern of the other infections people with AIDS can get.

"*Immunodeficiency* is a little harder to explain. Your **immune system** is sort of like your own built-in Superman. It's always there, fighting off things like viruses which are always trying to attack your body. It in-cludes special cells called **T** and **B cells** in your blood and lymph glands which are part of your defenses.

"The virus which causes AIDS knocks out your immune system—like kryptonite knocks out Superman. It kills most of your T cells, which makes your immune system deficient, or less effective. That's where the word *immunodeficiency* comes from," he said, pointing to the board. "Without your immune system, you can get all sorts of other infections."

Mr. Rutherford spent the next hour telling us about AIDS. He said that so far, most of the people who get AIDS are homosexuals, or people who have sexual intercourse with other people of the same sex. Another group of AIDS victims includes people who inject themselves with illegal drugs. "I doubt that Tommy qualifies as either a homosexual or a drug abuser."

One of the things he said was that lymph glands

swell up during any kind of infection, such as a cold, strep throat, or measles, not just AIDS. I guess that is why Mary wondered if I had AIDS. Now I'm happy that I just had a strep throat.

Facts about Infections

An **infection** occurs when part of your body is attacked by organisms, or living things, so tiny that a microscope is needed to see them. There are only four main types of organisms which cause infections. *Parasites* cause diseases such as malaria, which is rare in this country. *Fungi* cause problems such as athlete's foot. *Bacteria*, which are ten times smaller than fungi, cause strep throat and ear infections. Antibiotics are medicines like penicillin that are used to kill bacteria. *Viruses*, which are one hundred times smaller than bacteria, cause colds, mumps, measles, herpes, and AIDS. Your immune system can kill cold, mumps, and measles viruses. This is good because doctors have very few medicines which can kill viruses.

Unfortunately, your immune system is not very good at killing the virus which causes AIDS. This virus was first called *HTLV-III* or *LAV* virus. Now it is called the *human immunodeficiency virus* or **HIV**. This virus weakens your immune system. By weakening the immune system, HIV makes it difficult for people infected with this virus to fight off other infections.

A virus or bacterium is not the same thing as a disease. A **disease** is the group of problems caused by an organism when it attacks your body: fever, headache, sneezing, and so forth. You can have a virus in your body without having the disease it causes.

The difference between a virus and a disease is like the difference between a match and fire. The HIV virus can sit harmlessly in your body like a match in a box. If the HIV virus comes to life, like a match, the fire it causes can burn you up. However, only about one of every four people who carry HIV will develop AIDS.

How are infections spread?

When a virus or other type of organism attacks your body, you have been infected with that organism. The process of spreading the virus and the infection caused by the virus is called **transmission**.

Different types of viruses are transmitted in different ways. Viruses such as the chicken pox virus are transmitted when someone infected with the virus sneezes. There are lots of viruses in the sneeze. When you breathe near where someone has just sneezed, you may breathe in some of the virus and may become infected. The AIDS virus is not transmitted by sneezing. You cannot catch it from a sneeze or by shaking hands or sharing towels with someone infected with it. You can only catch the HIV virus if it is put directly into your blood—by a needle, by sexual intercourse with someone infected with the virus, or by a bite from an infected person that breaks your skin.

2
Different Folks

After finishing dessert, Dad left the table to watch the nightly news. How boring. Not that I like clearing the table and helping Mom with the dishes more than watching the news. But my ears perked up when Dan Rather said something about "gay rights activists."

"What's '**gay**'?" I asked Mom and Dad.

"Where did our eight-year-old come up with that question?" Mom said.

I didn't care about the news, but what Dan Rather said had reminded me of something that had happened that day. "Well, when I missed catching a kickball during gym today, Herbie started calling me 'Gay-Jay,'" I said.

"Something like this was bound to happen sooner or later. You and your friends wouldn't call each other names if you knew what they meant," said Dad.

"C'mon, Dad. It's just in fun," I said.

"I bet you didn't think that it was fun at the time," he answered.

"Oh, Dad, don't lecture. Just tell me what 'gay' means," I pleaded.

"OK. It's the same as *faggot* or *homo*," he said.

"Martin!" said Mom, "I don't want you adding such words to Jay's vocabulary."

"Now, Mildred, I'm sorry, but he's going to learn all these words anyway, so why not now?" Dad said. "I suppose you would prefer that I use the word *homosexual* instead."

"So gay, faggot, homo, and homosexual all mean the same thing? Wow! But what do they mean?" I repeated.

"The only way to tell you is with a lecture," said Mom.

"That's OK. I want to hear it," I said.

"Well," said Dad, "this subject is more important than the news." He turned off the television, Mom put down the dishes, and then we were back at the dining room table.

Mom and Dad looked at each other nervously. "You start," they said to each other at the same time.

"What's the big deal?" I asked.

"Jay, it's hard to talk about certain things, particularly when they have to do with feelings that men and women have for each other, or that people of the same sex have for each other," said Mom.

Dad started chewing his fingernails, a sure sign

that he was nervous. "Everyone has friends. If two friends are particularly special, especially if they love each other, as your mother and I do, they often get married. They live together and sleep together. Once that happens, they might also make children such as you."

"I bet that's what having sex means," I chimed in.

"You're pretty bright," said Dad, "but the formal name is **sexual intercourse** rather than *sex*. To answer your big question, your mother and I are called **heterosexuals** because I'm attracted to your mother, a woman, and she's attracted to me, a man. Men who prefer to have sexual intercourse with women, and women who prefer to have sexual intercourse with men, are heterosexual. Now, a **homosexual** is someone who prefers to have sexual contact with someone of the same sex."

Now I was getting nervous. "But all of my best friends are boys. Does that mean that Herbie was right to call me Gay-Jay?" I asked.

"Not at all," said Mom, smiling. "Everyone has both male and female friends. Pretty soon you're going to want to spend more time with the girls."

This lecture was getting pretty interesting. "Do homosexuals act and look different than heterosexuals?" I asked.

It was Dad's turn to answer. "Some people think that male homosexuals act a bit feminine, you know, like girls. Some people think that female homosexuals or **lesbians** act a bit like men. That may be true sometimes, but it's a pretty stupid thing to say because usually it's not true. For example, Burt, the mailman, is gay."

"That's impossible. He's a big, muscular guy. I'd never call him gay," I said.

"You shouldn't call him any name at all, but he's still a homosexual," said Dad. Then he got up to turn the TV back on.

"So you mean that anyone could be a homosexual?" I asked. Dad turned the TV up, meaning that the lecture was about to end.

"Well, only one in ten people is a homosexual," he said.

"One more question?" I asked.

"One short one," Dad answered.

"I heard one of the teachers say something about homosexuals and something called AIDS. What's that?" I asked.

"Another lecture," said Dad.

Facts about Sexuality

Jay learned that most people are attracted to members of the opposite sex and are called *heterosexuals*. Another word for heterosexual is *straight*. Those people who are attracted to members of the same sex are called *homosexuals*. While there are many words for homosexuals, the only ones which should be used are *gay*, for any homosexual, or *lesbian*, for homosexual women.

Is homosexuality normal?

While there are many more straight than gay people, there are probably twenty million gay people in the United States. Because there are so many gay people, it is reasonable to say that homosexuality is not abnormal. Homosexuals work, play, and have feelings just as heterosexuals do, but they prefer to have sexual contact with people of the same sex.

Will I become a homosexual?

No one can answer that question for you. You may have been born with a tendency to become homosexual or heterosexual. What happens to you as you grow up may also affect whether you become gay or straight.

It is normal to be attracted to someone of the same sex. Your best friend is probably the same sex as you. This doesn't mean you are homosexual. Most people become more interested in persons of the opposite sex after they reach the age of twelve or thirteen. Although a boy's best friends are still boys, he may begin to think of girls as cute. Girls may begin to talk to each other about the boys they like. However, other people become more interested in persons of their own sex. Those people are likely to become homosexuals.

What is the connection between homosexuals and AIDS?

People catch the HIV virus by having sexual intercourse or sexual contact with someone who is infected with the virus. The HIV virus which causes AIDS began in Africa. There, AIDS occurs equally among heterosexuals and homosexuals. It appears that some male homosexuals caught the HIV virus in Africa and brought it back to North America. Those men had sexual contact with other homosexuals in the United States, and the virus was quickly passed to more than half of the male homosexuals in the country. Therefore, it was believed that only homosexuals would develop AIDS. The HIV virus and AIDS have now begun to spread among heterosexuals and it is clear that an infected heterosexual can also spread the HIV virus through heterosexual intercourse.

Will everyone infected with the HIV virus develop AIDS?

Scientists do not know yet. It is estimated that at least one in four, and perhaps as many as seven in ten people infected with the HIV virus will develop AIDS.

When someone is infected with the HIV virus, the virus can be found inside his or her body and that person is said to **carry** the virus. Unfortunately, once someone is infected with the HIV virus, he or she will always carry the virus. Most people who are infected with the virus do not become sick for a long time, sometimes years. Infected people may not know that they are infected. These infected people may pass the virus to uninfected people through sexual contact, thus continuing the spread of AIDS.

Will I become gay if I spend time with someone who is gay?

Many people, both children and adults, think that they might become gay if they are around someone who is gay. There is no reason for this fear. You cannot become homosexual merely by spending time with someone who is. Homosexuality or hetero-sexuality is something that comes from inside you and from who you are, not from who you know.

3
Andy's
Appendix

Andy was never sick. He was Amity's star quarterback and a tough player. Now in the last quarter of the football game with Derby High School, Andy called a time-out and limped to the sidelines. He was sick to his stomach. Coach Johnson hurried to his side. "What's wrong, Andy? Were you kicked in the stomach?"

"I don't think so, Coach," replied Andy. "I didn't feel quite right at the beginning of the game. You know, a little out of it, no big deal. Now, my belly aches all over and I feel like throwing up." Andy turned pale and threw up behind the bench.

His parents quickly came down from the stands. They decided to take Andy to the hospital. As they started to the car, Lance Satler wished Andy well. This was Lance's chance to take Andy's place at quarterback.

Andy felt weaker and weaker on the way to the hospital. He was quickly put in a room while his parents registered at the emergency room desk. Twenty minutes later, Dr. Hahn called Andy's parents from the waiting room. "Andy has appendicitis," she said firmly. "He needs an operation this afternoon."

"What's appendicitis?" asked Andy.

"Well," said Dr. Hahn, "An 'itis' is a kind of inflammation or swelling. And your appendix is part of your intestine. When your appendix gets inflamed, you have appendicitis. When that happens, the appendix has to come out. That's why you need an operation. It's a routine operation," said Dr. Hahn, looking at Andy's parents. "He will have a small scar on the right side of his belly. He'll be able to go home in a couple of days."

"When can I play football again? The state championship is in three weeks," Andy said.

"Football, hmm. We'll have to wait a little on that one," the doctor said.

Andy's mother spoke up. "I do have one concern," she said. "Will Andy need a **transfusion**?"

"What's a transfusion?" asked Andy.

"When you lose a lot of blood, like in some operations or accidents, you need to have the lost blood replaced.

That's called a transfusion," said Dr. Hahn.

"Where does the blood come from?" asked Andy.

"From someone who donated a little of their own blood," said Dr. Hahn.

"Could Andy catch AIDS from a blood transfusion?" asked Andy's mother.

"Not a chance," Dr. Hahn replied. "Some cases of AIDS were caused by blood transfusion. However, a new blood test makes it almost impossible to catch AIDS from a transfusion."

"I'm not having any operation if it could give me AIDS. The nurses have already poked me with needles to draw blood from me. Could that give me AIDS? Then they put this plastic needle and tube in my arm," said Andy, pointing to the hanging bottle of clear liquid and the tube that led from it to his arm. "I'm getting out, even if my stomach kills me. I'm not going to catch AIDS."

Dr. Hahn stared Andy straight in the eye. "Andy, you can't catch AIDS from being poked or prodded in the hospital. All of the needles we've stuck you with were used only once—on you. You can only catch the AIDS virus from a needle if that needle has been used by somebody with the AIDS virus. You can't catch AIDS by donating blood or by giving blood samples, as you have done. You can only catch it if you get infected blood from someone else. Even if I had AIDS, I couldn't give it to you by talking to you or by examining you with my hands or stethoscope."

Looking towards Andy's parents, Dr. Hahn said,

"It's amazing how often parents and their kids ask about AIDS instead of asking more important questions about the operation. It is not possible for us to give patients AIDS. Is that clear?"

"Well, OK," said Andy's mother.

"Now that that's settled, let's get to the operating room," said Dr. Hahn.

Two hours later, Dr. Hahn talked to Andy and his parents in his hospital room. Andy was still groggy from the medicine they had given him to make him sleep through the operation. "Andy's appendix is out and the whole operation went very smoothly."

"That's wonderful," replied Andy's mother. "Did he need a transfusion?"

Dr. Hahn put her hands on her hips. "Still concerned about AIDS, aren't you? Well, not only did Andy not need a transfusion, he hardly lost any blood at all."

"Can friends come by? Did we win the game?" Andy asked.

Andy's father said, "How do you expect us to know who won the game when we've been with you the whole time? And your friends will have to wait. Why don't you just sleep until tomorrow?"

The next morning, Andy's nurse came in and opened the curtains onto a bright, cloudless fall day. "You can't sleep through a beautiful day like this one. Besides, a friend of yours by the name of Lance is here to see you."

Lance strolled into the room carrying a plastic bag under his arm like a football. "So, Superman, how did the appendix go?" he asked. As he opened the bag, Lance added, "By the way, I brought you a present from the game. The best quarterback in the league certainly deserves it."

Andy's eyes lit up. It was the football from yesterday's game. The whole team had signed it and someone had written in the final score. Amity had won, 24 to 21.

Facts about Transfusions

Andy's parents were almost as worried about their son getting AIDS from a blood transfusion as they were about his appendix. There is now a test which can tell doctors whether blood is infected with AIDS. This means that hospitals can keep infected blood out of the **blood bank**.

If someone is very ill or needs an operation, their family should concern themselves with the illness, not with the transfusion or the chance of getting AIDS.

What is a transfusion?

A transfusion is the transfer of any liquid, such as blood or a special salt water called *saline*, into your bloodstream. Usually a special plastic tube with a needle in the end is used to transfer the liquid from a bottle into your blood. The tube is called an **intra-venous** line, meaning that the line goes into a vein, where blood is flowing.

When is a blood transfusion needed?

Sometimes a person loses a lot of blood in a short time, such as after a bad car accident or during surgery. Then the person cannot make new blood quickly enough to meet his or her body's needs. At times such as these, a blood transfusion is needed.

Are blood and saline the only things injected into the bloodstream?

Blood and saline are only two of many things given intravenously. Many medicines can also be put directly into the blood. Medicines given in this way work much faster than pills which are swallowed.

Unfortunately, some people inject themselves with certain illegal medicines or drugs because they think it feels good. These people are called *intravenous drug abusers*. **Drug abusers** sometimes use needles that are not clean to inject themselves or their friends. When several people use the same needle, any disease that one of the people has can spread to the others. A dirty needle can put germs for diseases like AIDS or hepatitis, a liver disease, right into the blood.

How is blood tested for AIDS to make sure it is safe for transfusion?

Since 1985, a good, but not perfect, blood test has been used to identify blood which might have the AIDS virus in it. Infected blood is not used for transfusions. When a person is infected with the AIDS virus, his or her immune system makes a special chemical called an **antibody** which tries to destroy the virus. The test detects the presence of these antibodies. The test does not detect the virus itself. In the near future, a better test, one that detects the AIDS virus itself, will be used to make the blood supply perfectly safe.

4
Adding
Insult to Injury

When the bus got to school, a bunch of parents would not let me in the school door. It had never bothered me until they tried to keep me out of school. "It" was **hemophilia** and "they" were a group of parents who felt that I might give their kids AIDS.

It wasn't my fault that I had hemophilia. I was born with it.

The doctors said that hemophilia is one of many **inherited diseases**. An inherited disease is one that you get from your parents, even if they do not appear to have the disease.

When most people get hurt they get a bruise, which means that they have bled inside their skin. Your body makes many **proteins** to control how much you bleed. They go together to make blood clots that close off cuts or stop bruises from swelling. If you have hemophilia, one of these proteins is missing and when you're bruised you keep bleeding and bleeding.

The doctors cannot cure hemophilia, but they can help control it by putting the missing protein into your blood so your body can stop the bleeding. My blood is missing a protein called Factor VIII. I think that everyone in the world except me makes his own Factor VIII. Since I don't make any, I have to get it from other people. Whenever someone donates blood, the Factor VIII is removed. A batch of Factor VIII contains the protein from many different people.

The problem is this stupid AIDS virus. Before blood was tested for the AIDS virus, the virus snuck into my batch of Factor VIII. Then it was transfused into me. Even though I'm not gay, or a drug abuser, the types of people who usually catch AIDS, I'm infected with the AIDS virus.

And these crazy parents want to keep me out of school.

Mr. Foley, the principal, walked around the group of parents and met me as I got off the school bus. "Steve, let's walk around to the gym and go in the side entrance," he said.

"I don't want to do that, Mr. Foley. That would be giving in to these parents," I said.

"Well, I'll stay with you until the police come and break up the crowd. We called them already," he said.

My best friend Robby stayed with me too. "Steve, you don't even *have* AIDS, just that pre-AIDS thing, right?" he asked.

"Yes. The doctors call it *ARC*, short for **AIDS-related complex**," I replied. "They figured out that I had it when I had swollen lymph glands—remember? I had all those little bumps on my neck."

"I thought they were kind of neat. But I guess your mom and dad were worried about it being AIDS," Robby said. "How did they figure out that it wasn't ?"

"Because people who really have AIDS hardly ever get better. They catch all sorts of other things. You know, I haven't even had a cold for a year," I answered.

"You're probably cured, huh?"

"Well, not exactly," I said. "The doctors think that I'll never get the AIDS disease but they don't know for sure. I'll probably always be infected with the AIDS virus."

Robby came up with his idea of a brilliant idea. "Why don't you just spit or cough on one of those people. Boy, I bet that would break up the crowd fast! They'd think that you had given them AIDS."

"That's the problem," I replied. As I was talking, I could hear the police siren coming up the school driveway. "They really think that spitting or something like that will spread AIDS. It just isn't true."

I never had a chance to spit. Not that I intended to. The police came and broke up the crowd of parents. Some of them shouted something about "going to court" to keep me out of school. The other kids from the bus cheered when the police put handcuffs on the two loudest parents. I didn't want to think about it. At least for one more day, I got to go to class.

Facts about Hemophilia

Steve has hemophilia. It is an uncommon disease. People with hemophilia are called *hemophiliacs*. When a normal person gets a cut or a bruise, certain parts of the blood team up to stop the bleeding, making a blood clot. Hemophiliacs are missing one of the parts of blood which makes blood clot. This part has to be supplied by transfusions.

Are transfusions dangerous?

When someone gives blood, he or she is called a **blood donor**. The donated blood is given to patients who need blood. Sometimes a blood donor is infected with a virus which lives in the blood. Two examples of viruses which live in the blood are hepatitis, which causes liver disease, and the HIV virus, which causes AIDS. Viruses cannot be removed from donor blood. Therefore, a person receiving infected blood could develop hepatitis or AIDS. A blood transfusion from an infected donor would be considered dangerous.

Can infected blood be found before it is used?

Blood is now tested before it is transfused to make sure that it will not cause AIDS or hepatitis.

Can hemophilia be cured?

There is no cure for hemophilia yet. However, scientists have recently been able to make Factor VIII in the laboratory. In a few years, most hemophiliacs will receive Factor VIII made in the laboratory. They won't have to worry about the danger of transfusions anymore.

Do many hemophiliacs have AIDS?

More than nine out of ten hemophiliacs have been infected with the HIV virus by receiving transfusions of Factor VIII which contained the virus. A few of these people have developed AIDS. Of those infected with the HIV virus, more than one in four will eventually develop AIDS and is likely to die from it. The other infected hemophiliacs will carry the virus forever but not be ill.

What is ARC?

ARC stands for *AIDS-related complex*. People with ARC are infected with the AIDS virus but do not have AIDS. ARC refers to a number of medical problems which occur in these people. Many but not all people with ARC will eventually have AIDS.

5
Getting High

"What are they doing in there?" Greg whispered to Duncan, his best friend. Duncan was peeping through the keyhole into his brother Spencer's bedroom.

"I bet they're doing something illegal, but I can't tell yet. It's pretty dark in there," Duncan whispered back.

The bedroom was lit only by a few small candles. Duncan could smell incense burning. Spencer had his sleeves rolled up and his girlfriend Tina was tying something around his arm. Duncan did not know who the other man in the room was, but he looked meaner than Rambo. "I bet they're doing drugs," said Greg.

Spencer had been using drugs for two years, against his parents' wishes. They said he was mixed up with a bad crowd. Each time they threatened to kick him out of the house, Spencer promised he would quit using drugs. And each time, he started to use drugs again.

His parents thought that if they really threw him out of the house, they would never see him again. Certainly he wouldn't finish high school. The police had come over and arrested him twice.

Duncan remembered the first arrest very clearly. His brother had come home with a new stereo system and his father had asked where he got the money to pay for it. Spencer just kept saying that he got the stereo from a friend. His father called the police because Spencer would not return it. Spencer had been arrested the second time for beating someone up.

"It's my turn to look," said Greg.

"They had better not see us, or we're in for real trouble," said Duncan. "Quiet."

"Duncan, it looks like the big guy is heating up a needle in the candle. And—now Tina is sticking it in Spencer's arm. Yow, that must hurt. He's not even flinching," whispered Greg excitedly.

"Shhh," said Duncan. "It's my turn to look again."

Sure enough, the needle was in Spencer's arm. The fellow who looked liked Rambo was injecting something into Spencer's arm. Duncan thought he could hear his brother say something about "feeling good." It certainly didn't look like it felt good. Then it was Tina's turn. The band which had been around Spencer's arm was tied around Tina's arm and Spencer was heating up the needle again.

"I can't believe that they're using the same needle," Greg said. "I won't even drink from the same glass as my brother, and Tina is using the same old needle

Spencer used. They didn't even wash it or anything."

"They call it *getting high*," said Duncan.

"I don't know about getting high, but they're going to get all sorts of germs," said Greg.

There was some movement in the room. Before Duncan and Greg could get away from the door, Spencer had opened it and was glaring down at them. Duncan escaped downstairs and out the door but Spencer grabbed Greg by the arm. He growled, "If I ever catch you sneaking around here again, it will be the last time you're alive."

Greg wriggled free. He was still shaking when he caught up with Duncan outside. "Did you see the look in his eyes?" said Duncan. "It was horrible. It's like he's not really there."

"Boy, that was close," said Greg. "Are you going to tell your mom and dad?"

"I don't know. I'm really afraid to say anything but I know I should. What would you do?" asked Duncan.

Facts about Drug Abuse

There are several ways people can put drugs into their bodies. Drugs can be swallowed, smoked, sniffed up the nose, or injected into the blood with a needle.

Most drugs are medicines used to treat illnesses. Some drugs are used by people who are not sick. These people like the feeling that they get from using the drug. Using drugs just to change the way you feel, not to make you well, is called *drug abuse*.

Any drug can be abused. Some people take too many vitamins. Many of the drugs which are abused are illegal to have. The drugs which cause the greatest problems include alcohol, heroin, and cocaine. Even though drinking alcohol is legal, many people drink too much. When alcohol is abused, it accounts for many fights at home and car accidents on the road.

What is a drug overdose?

When someone takes more of a drug than his or her body can handle at one time, that person has taken an overdose. Overdoses of heroin or cocaine often cause heart attacks, even in young people. Overdoses of some drugs can kill people.

Are street drugs dangerous?

Street drugs are so-called because they are sold "on the street," by someone who is not licensed to sell drugs. Someone who sells street drugs is called a *dealer*. Pharmacists, who work at drug stores or in hospitals, are licensed to sell drugs which have been ordered by a doctor. Street drugs are much more dangerous than medicines ordered by a doctor because there is no way to know exactly what is in a street drug. For example, pure cocaine is never sold by a dealer. Cocaine sold on the street is diluted with something else—sugar, cornstarch, or even another drug. The user has no way of knowing what these extra ingredients are, and no way of knowing exactly how much pure drug he or she is getting.

Can germs be passed by intravenous drug needles?

Absolutely yes. This problem is of great concern because dangerous diseases, such as the virus which causes AIDS, are spread by **contaminated** needles. More than one-half of the people who abuse intravenous drugs are now infected with the HIV virus and many will develop AIDS and die.

If drug abuse is so dangerous, why do people abuse drugs?

People who abuse drugs usually do not realize that the drugs are causing any problem. Some people use drugs as a way to escape from everyday life. When they are high, they forget their problems for a while. Others use drugs because their friends do. Many people use drugs because they like the way drugs make them feel. One problem with all of these reasons is that many drugs are addictive. This means that once people have taken a drug, and liked the way it made them feel, they want to take it again and again. Some people need more and more drugs to make them feel good, until *not* taking the drug makes them feel awful. Drugs can be very expensive, and drug abusers may have to steal to pay for their expensive habit. A second problem is the fact that all drugs have side effects which can be dangerous. Drug abusers often die from an overdose.

6
Stefan's Story:
A Life
Cut Short

I could not possibly have been happier. I was in my sophomore year of college and everything was going well. Swim team practice had been hard at first but now I was in good enough shape so that it was almost fun. Workouts were much harder here than they had been in high school, where I had been the captain of the team. All of my classes were great, especially Russian history and English literature. Best of all was my social life.

In high school, all my buddies went out with girls. I did too, but only because it was the thing to do. I was never really attracted

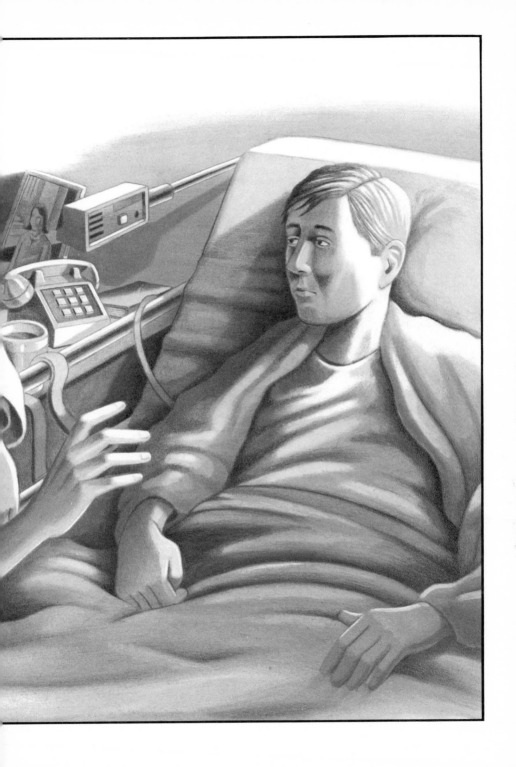

to girls as much as I was attracted to some of the guys. I thought then that I might be a homosexual. In college, I finally had the chance to find others who felt the same way. My best buddy on the team, George Adler, and I would go to a gay club downtown and have sexual intercourse with other gays.

It was one of those things my mom and dad could never possibly understand. They are so straight. My little sister, Melissa, was telling me how she was just getting interested in guys. She would never believe that I was more interested in them than she was. I don't know why I am. I've heard someone compare it to being left-handed—some people are just born that way.

Because of the AIDS epidemic, George and I had thought about not going to the gay club anymore. We worried about catching AIDS, but we thought it would never happen to either of us.

I was wrong.

One day in the locker room after swim practice, I noticed something strange. "Hey, George, what is this white stuff in my mouth?" I asked.

George came over and looked as I bent my head back. "I don't know, but it looks pretty strange. You'd better check it out."

At the student health center, Dr. Ramsay was very concerned. In fact, he had me scared stiff. He asked questions about how I felt and my homosexual habits. He said the white stuff in my mouth was a kind of fungus called *thrush* or *Candida*. Then he added the bad news. He said that this infection was common in people with AIDS and some other conditions.

Under my arm and in my neck he found swollen lymph glands, another change that can happen to AIDS or ARC patients.

"What are these blue spots on my arms?" I asked. "I noticed them about a month ago."

He looked even more concerned. He put on a pair of gloves to touch them.

"Stefan," he said, "if it's OK with you, I'm going to numb one of these spots with Novocain and then cut it out to send to the laboratory."

"If that's the right thing to do, that's fine with me, Dr. Ramsay," I said. It hardly hurt and it took less than ten minutes. He said I would have to wait a week for the result of the test on the skin.

"Do I have AIDS?" I asked.

"We really don't know yet. What this little piece of skin looks like under the microscope will be very important," replied Dr. Ramsay.

The week of waiting for the test result was the worst week of my life. I couldn't eat or sleep. I couldn't study. The swimming coach wanted to know why I had lost all of my energy. George was as scared as I was — both for me and for himself.

Dr. Ramsay's news was bad. "The blue spots are Kaposi's sarcoma. That's a kind of cancer that AIDS patients get."

I had AIDS.

My thoughts were whirling. Could I be treated?

How long would I live? Would I suffer? What else would I catch?

I already knew most of the answers. I just couldn't believe they actually applied to me.

Dr. Ramsay must have known what I was thinking. "The list of illnesses that AIDS patients get becomes longer almost every day," he said. "They include a kind of *tuberculosis* or infection of the lung, another lung disease called *pneumocystis carinii*, *dementia* or confusion and loss of memory, infections of the brain, and certain kinds of cancer."

"It sounds like a bad science fiction movie, with me the victim," I said.

"Stefan, as you know, there are no cures yet. You could live anywhere from one month to three years. It just depends," he said.

"Depends on what?"

Dr. Ramsay had a one-word answer. "Luck."

First they took an X-ray. Then they took some of my blood for a series of tests. One test was to look for antibodies to the HIV virus. Another test was to learn something about my immune system by seeing how many **suppressor** and **helper T cells** I had in my bloodstream. These cells in the bloodstream are an important part of the immune system. The helper T cells help fight infections while the suppressor T cells tell the helper T cells when the fight is over. In patients with AIDS, the helper T cells are killed by the HIV virus. When that happens, the immune system cannot fight infections.

I had only spent the afternoon in the clinic, but leaving it was like being freed from jail and having nowhere to go.

I thought about killing myself before AIDS could kill me, but I decided it would be too easy to give in. I had to try to fight.

I would be going home for Thanksgiving in two days. I had to say something at home. I decided that I would just be honest and tell the family.

I made my announcement at Thanksgiving dinner. It sure put a damper over everyone. I felt like a leper in my own home. Even Melissa was afraid to talk to me or touch me. I couldn't wait to leave home and let them think about it without me there.

When I saw George, back at college, it was like I had lost my best friend. We couldn't talk to each other because he knew that he was also probably going to get AIDS.

I had a long talk with the swim coach. We decided that if I wanted to continue practicing, it was fine with him, but we had to let the rest of the team know. After a team meeting, two of the guys quit. They thought that the pool was permanently infected. Everyone else was more realistic and thought that if I wanted to practice, that was fine. We decided that it would be best if I didn't swim in the meets because it might cause too many problems with the other teams.

When I returned home for Christmas break, things were much better. The whole family had a great trip to the Caribbean. The sun made me feel better. Melissa thought I was losing weight. I thought so, too. I was looking forward to the next semester of college, but I was afraid AIDS was getting the better of me.

I had to quit swim practice just before the end of the season in February because I was too weak. My teammates were great. They threw a "leave of absence" party for me even though we all knew that the leave would be permanent.

The next week, I started having trouble with my math class. Something was wrong. I had always been a whiz at math. Dr. Ramsay ordered a special X-ray of my head called a CAT scan. It showed that my brain was becoming smaller. I had AIDS dementia.

The week after that, I began to have trouble breathing. The clinic did a special test by putting a tube through my nose and into my lungs. More bad news. I had pneumocystis pneumonia.

The AIDS virus had wiped out my immune system.

I got worse every day after that until finally I couldn't leave the hospital. Lots of friends came by to say hello. They had a hard time finding something to say. I didn't know how to tell them that they didn't have to say anything. I just wanted them to be there.

A Life Cut Short

Stefan was only nineteen and very healthy before he developed AIDS. It is not uncommon for this deadly virus to cause so many problems so quickly.

An illness such as AIDS causes problems for the victim and for his or her family and friends. Although

Stefan was pretty independent before he developed AIDS, after he became sick he needed his family and friends more than ever.

How long does someone with AIDS live?

Once a diagnosis of AIDS is made, the person may live anywhere from one month to three or even six years.

Is there a cure for AIDS?

There is no cure for AIDS yet. To cure AIDS, ways are needed to kill the AIDS virus and reverse the diseases the people with AIDS get. Many scientists are trying to find medicines which will kill the AIDS virus. Other scientists are trying to figure out how to rebuild the immune system once it has been weakened by the AIDS virus.

Can AIDS be treated or controlled?

People with AIDS can have many illnesses, including, for example, rashes or infections. Doctors can give medicines to treat these rashes or infections. If the medicine works, the rash or infection goes away and the person has been treated successfully. If the medicine only prevents the rash or infection from getting worse, then the illness has been controlled. Unfortunately, there are no good treatments for some of the illnesses that people with AIDS get. When these illnesses get out of control, the person eventually dies.

7
Melissa's Story:
A Brother with AIDS

I will always remember last Thanksgiving dinner. My oldest brother, Stefan, was coming home from college and I had missed him. I was so proud of him. He was kind of an idol to me. My girlfriends always asked me what it was like to live with such a handsome brother. He had been captain of the high school swimming team. Everyone adored him.

When he said at the beginning of dinner that he had an announcement to make, I blurted out, "I bet you finally have a girlfriend."

My other brother, Eric kicked me under the table, saying, "Quiet, Melissa. Can't you give someone else a chance to talk? We get to see and hear you all the time. We haven't seen Stefan in almost three months."

I stuck my tongue out at Eric, but I forgot all about him when I heard Stefan's announcement.

Stefan looked right at Mom and Dad. In his quiet voice, the one he used when he was being very serious, he said, "Mom, Dad, there are two things I have to tell you. It's not a reflection on you and I don't want you to be mad at me. If anything, I need your support. I don't know if you ever suspected it, but I am gay. I've known it for years. The second thing is, I have AIDS."

I wasn't sure if Daddy was going to drop the turkey knife or use it on someone. The hurt in Mom's and Dad's eyes was unbelievable. My mom covered her eyes and burst into tears, saying, "What did we do wrong? How could this happen to our son?"

No one could look at Stefan. My brother couldn't possibly be gay. It was as if a plague had been sent to the house. Dinner ended before it even started.

In the weeks after Thanksgiving, we all began to get used to it. Stefan was gay and he had AIDS. Getting mad at him or ourselves would not help anything. As usual, Stefan was right. We decided that we needed to support him, not shy away from him. Dad said that a trip to the Caribbean during Christmas vacation would be best for everyone.

When we finally started thinking again, we had so many questions. Was it safe to be in the same house as Stefan? Could we use dishes that he used? Could we use the same bathroom and toothpaste? Could I touch him? Could I hug and kiss him hello? Stefan's doctor assured us that the answer to all of the questions was "Yes." He insisted that the only way we could catch AIDS was from a dirty needle or from sex with someone infected with the AIDS virus. That was something I did not want to think about. I couldn't understand how Stefan could like other boys or think they were cute, the same way I did.

Christmas dinner went much better than Thanksgiving dinner. Things weren't quite the same as before, but everyone was happy to see Stefan again. We had tons of presents.

The next day we left for the Caribbean. On the beach I got back some of my summer tan. Stefan was swimming as strongly as ever, but he looked like he'd lost some of his muscles. He told me that he hadn't been eating quite right because of final exams, but that he would put the weight back on.

He never did. In March, the doctor called from the big hospital near Stefan's college to say that Stefan was very ill. The next day we drove the 200 miles to see him.

I could hardly recognize him. I didn't want to touch him. There were all sorts of lights and machines in the room and tubes going in and out of my brother. When I talked to him, his answers didn't make sense. He was always short of breath. A young woman doctor said Stefan's brain had also been affected by the AIDS virus, which was why he couldn't think right. She called it a kind of dementia.

"What's wrong with his breathing?" I asked.

She put her arm around me, saying, "Let's talk outside."

We sat down in the lounge and she continued, "Stefan has a kind of pneumonia that AIDS patients often get. That's why he has trouble breathing."

"But can't you make it go away?" I asked.

"Usually not. Antibiotics are not very useful against this bacteria. Besides, his immune system is not helping fight diseases at all. The AIDS virus has destroyed it."

"What about those blue spots on his arms and face?"

"That's something else that occurs just about only in AIDS patients. It's a rare kind of skin cancer called Kaposi's sarcoma," she answered.

"Can you cure that?" I asked.

"No, Melissa. We can't. Not yet."

I started to cry. "How could this horrible thing be happening to my brother? AIDS, dementia, pneumonia, and cancer. He's only nineteen! And you doctors can't cure any of it?"

"We're working on it. But there is a long way to go," she answered sadly.

My perfect brother, Stefan, died three days later. It was a long ride home.

Facts about AIDS

AIDS can strike any family. It does not choose between rich and poor or black and white. It is a disease which has mostly affected homosexuals who have had sexual contact with many different people. Many intravenous drug abusers have been infected by dirty needles. Heterosexuals who have had sexual intercourse with many different people are also more likely to get AIDS. A few people, including most hemophiliacs, were infected by contaminated transfusions before there were tests to help screen out infected blood.

Where did AIDS come from?

The HIV virus which causes AIDS appears to have originated in the middle of Africa. Many people in Africa have developed AIDS. In Africa, most of the infections occur in heterosexuals, not homosexuals. There are other viruses in Africa which are similar to the HIV virus. One of these, called HIV-II, infects people and also causes AIDS. Another infects African green monkeys but does not give them AIDS.

Is it safe to be around someone with AIDS?

It appears to be safe to be around someone with AIDS. Shaking hands or sharing dishes with someone with AIDS, or living in the same house or even using the same toothbrush as someone with AIDS has never been shown to pass the disease. Sexual intercourse is known to transmit AIDS.

Should children with AIDS be allowed to go to school with other children?

It might be possible for an infected person to transmit AIDS to an uninfected person by biting hard enough to break the skin and cause bleeding. However, as long as a child with AIDS is mature enough not to bite other children, it is safe for such a child to be with other children.

How do children get AIDS?

Some children got AIDS from blood transfusions before there were tests to sort out infected blood. A much greater concern is the passing of the AIDS or HIV virus from a pregnant mother to her unborn child. Most women who abuse intravenous drugs are infected with the HIV virus. Babies share some body fluids with their mothers until they are born, so mothers can transmit diseases to their unborn children. Most babies from mothers infected with the HIV virus are born infected. Many of the infected babies will develop AIDS and die before their second birthday.

Can AIDS be prevented?

Many scientists are working on a **vaccine** to prevent AIDS. At present, the only way to prevent it is to avoid situations in which you could catch it, such as intravenous drug use with contaminated needles, or sexual contact with an infected person. Although mosquitos are known to transmit a few diseases in a way similar to the way sharing an intravenous needle does, there is no evidence that mosquitos have transmitted the AIDS virus.

Do condoms prevent the spread of AIDS?

A **condom** is a special rubber balloon that can be

placed over a man's penis at the time of sexual intercourse. It forms a thin barrier between a man and his sexual partner. Condoms are used to prevent a woman from becoming pregnant or to prevent the spread of diseases which can be transmitted by sexual intercourse. The use of a condom decreases the chance that a man infected with the AIDS virus will spread the virus during sexual intercourse. The use of a condom might also decrease the man's risk of catching the AIDS virus from his sexual partner.

Has anyone with AIDS been cured?

No. On the other hand, many powerful new medicines are being tested in patients with AIDS. The names of some of them are *interferon, interleukin II, ribavarin, GM-CSF,* and *azidothymidine* or *AZT,* also called *zidovudine.* If we continue to quickly learn so much about AIDS and the AIDS virus, there is hope in the future for a cure.

Facts about the Future

It was thought at first that only homosexuals got AIDS. Now we know that anyone could get AIDS. In the United States, over one million men, women, and a few children are infected with the HIV virus which causes AIDS. About one in four of these will develop AIDS and probably die. The rest will remain infected for life and may or may not develop AIDS.

AIDS is still a new disease but it will be with us for a long time. In the short time that the AIDS epidemic has developed, we have learned a lot about the HIV virus. We have learned about how it spreads and the disease it causes, AIDS.

A vaccine to protect against the HIV virus has not yet been made. There also is no cure for AIDS. Therefore, the best way to protect yourself from the virus which causes AIDS is to avoid getting in a situation where you could catch it. These situations include sexual contact with someone infected with the AIDS virus, or sharing a needle with an infected person. AIDS cannot be caught by eating in a restaurant even if a cook there has the virus. AIDS cannot be caught by using a public toilet, even if someone with AIDS has used the same toilet.

There is a blood test which can reveal if someone is infected with the AIDS virus. This test may help prevent the spread of AIDS.

Through this book, you have learned who is at risk for catching AIDS. You have seen how difficult life is for an AIDS victim and his family. In real life you will meet people with AIDS. You should treat them with respect and not be afraid of them. You cannot catch AIDS by sharing your time with someone who has AIDS. You can make them feel less alone by showing that you care.

Resources

For more information about AIDS or for help if you or someone you know has AIDS, you can contact one of these organizations. They should also be able to tell you about organizations in your area that you can call.

The American Red Cross, 17th and D Streets NW, Washington, DC 20006. Telephone: (202) 637-8300. This is the national headquarters. The American Red Cross has offices in many cities. It has published a series of pamphlets on AIDS, and you can get these pamphlets and other information from your local American Red Cross.

Public Health Service, Department of Health and Human Services. AIDS Hotline: (800) 342-AIDS or (800) 342-2437.

National Association of People with AIDS, sponsored by the National Lesbian and Gay Health Foundation Inc., P.O. Box 65472, Washington, DC 20035. Telephone: (202) 797-3708.

National Gay Task Force, 80 Fifth Avenue, New York, NY 10011. AIDS Hotline: (800) 221-7044.

World Hemophilia AIDS Center, 2400 South Flower Street, Los Angeles, CA 90007. Telephone: (213) 742-1354.

Glossary

acquired immunodeficiency syndrome: an incurable disease caused by the HIV virus

AIDS: abbreviation of acquired immunodeficiency syndrome

AIDS-related complex (ARC): a group of problems or changes which people infected with the AIDS virus may have before they become so sick that they have the disease called AIDS

antibody: a protein made by B cells which helps fight infections

B cell: a cell which makes antibodies to fight infection

blood bank: a place where blood is stored until it is needed for transfusions

blood donor: a person who gives some of his or her blood to a blood bank or hospital

carrier: a person who is infected with an organism that could be transmitted to someone else

condom: a special rubber balloon that can be placed over a man's penis before sexual intercourse. It can prevent the spread of disease and keep his female partner from becoming pregnant

contaminate: to infect or make impure, especially with an organism

disease: a group of physical problems usually caused by an organism

drug abuser: a person who uses drugs to change the way he or she feels, not to make himself or herself well

gay: a homosexual

hemophilia: an inherited disease which makes people unable to stop bleeding when cut or bruised

heterosexual: someone who prefers a member of the opposite sex for romantic or sexual relationships

HIV: abbreviation for human immunodeficiency virus, the virus which causes AIDS

homosexual: someone who prefers a member of the same sex for romantic or sexual relationships

immune system: the combination of T cells, B cells and lymph glands that protects you from infections

infection: an invasion by organisms such as bacteria, fungi, or viruses

61

infectious: able to cause an infection

inherited disease: a disease you are born with, which your parents gave you just as they gave you the color of your hair. Your parents need not have the disease themselves

intravenous: inside a vein

lesbian: a woman who is sexually attracted to other women

lymph glands: small bumps in your body that help fight infections

protein: a compound in your body or food which is needed for normal growth and function

sexual contact: contact between people for sexual pleasure, especially touching of private parts

sexual intercourse: sexual contact involving the entry of a man's penis into his sexual partner's vagina or private parts

straight: a heterosexual

symptom: a physical change or feeling, such as a fever, that is different from normal and that doctors know to be a sign of disease

syndrome: a group of symptoms which occur together and indicate that someone has a certain disease

T cells: types of cell in the immune system which include *helper T cells*, which tell B cells to make antibodies, and *suppressor T cells*, which turn off helper T cells. The HIV virus attacks and kills helper T cells

transfusion: the transfer of a liquid such as blood or saline into the bloodstream

transmission: the process of spreading an organism and the infection caused by that organism

vaccine: medicine given to people by a doctor, usually by a shot, to prevent disease

vein: a tube in the body through which blood runs

virus: a very small organism that can cause an infection

Index